Buster Plays Along

by Marc Brown

LITTLE, BROWN AND COMPANY
New York Boston

Little, Brown and Company, Time Warner Book Group
1271 Avenue of the Americas, New York, NY 10020 • www.lb-kids.com
First Edition
Library of Congress Cataloging-in-Publication Data
Brown, Marc Tolon.
Buster plays along / Marc Brown.—1st ed. p. cm.—(Postcards from Buster)
Summary: Buster sends postcards to his friends back home when he and his father go to San Antonio, Texas for the International Accordian Festival.
ISBN 0-316-15886-0 (hc)/ISBN 0-316-00109-0 (pb)
[1. Accordian—Fiction. 2. Rabbits—Fiction. 3. Postcards—Fiction. 4. San Antonio (Tex.)—Fiction.] I. Title.
II. Brown, Marc Tolon. Postcards from Buster. PZ7.B81618Bm 2005 [E]—dc22 2004010272

Printed in the United States of America • 10 9 8 7 6 5 4 3 2 1

Cover left, right, and pages 3 and 11 top: Dave G. Houser, San Antonio Convention and Visitors Bureau; page 11 bottom: Al Rendon, San Antonio Convention and Visitors Bureau; pages 38-39 top two photos: Dave G. Houser, San Antonio Convention and Visitors Bureau; bottom photo: Al Rendon, San Antonio Convention and Visitors Bureau. Other photos from *Postcards from Buster* courtesy of WGBH Boston, and Cinar Productions, Inc. in association with Marc Brown Studios.

Do you know what these words MEAN?

Alamo: (Al-uh-mo) a large building in Texas that was originally a church

Bajo sexto: (bah-ho SEKS-toh) a twelve-string guitar from Mexico that usually plays the bass line of the music

Conjunto: (con-HUN-toh) A kind of music from the Texas-Mexico border region that has its roots in Mexico: Conjunto music is jazzy and energetic.

guacamole: (gwah-kuh-MOH-lay) a kind of Mexican food; the recipe can change from place to place, but it usually includes avocadoes, onions, limes, and hot pepper.

taco: (TAH-koh) a kind of Mexican food in which a flat pancake, called a **tortilla (tor-TEE-uh)** is wrapped around a filling

STATEtistics

San Antonio, Texas

- 9th largest city in US.
- Basketball team is San Antonio Spurs.
- Sea World San Antonio is the largest marine life park in the world.
- El Mercado is the largest Mexican marketplace outside of Mexico.

"Which cowboy hat
should I bring to San Antonio?"
Buster asked Arthur.

"I don't know," said Arthur.
"There might not be enough room."

Buster laughed.
"Texas is really big, Arthur."

"I didn't mean room in Texas,"
said Arthur.
"I meant room on the plane."

TEXAS

"You're bringing your accordion, too?"
Arthur asked.

Buster nodded.
"My dad and I are going to
the International Accordion Festival.
Maybe I'll decide to play, too."

TOLON
TEXAS
TRAVE
GUIDE

When Buster got to San Antonio,
he and his father
walked around the city.

"It looks like Mexico here," said Buster.

"That's because we're close to Mexico,"
Mr. Baxter explained.
"In fact, the city was
started by Mexican people."

Dear Arthur,

I went to visit the Alamo.
It was built as a mission
in 1718.

In 1836 a lot of brave men
tried to defend it
during a war with Mexico.

Texans have remembered
the Alamo ever since.

Buster

At a music festival,
Buster met Robert and his friend, Rudy.
They were both going to be playing in the accordion festival.

"It's great to introduce Conjunto music to someone new," said Rudy.

"What's that?" asked Buster.

"Ah," said Rudy.
"It's the music made when the accordion and this big guitar are played together.
The guitar is called a Bajo Sexto."

Dear Brain,

The accordion was invented in Austria in 1829—which you probably knew already.

It is often played here with a big guitar called a Bajo Sexto.

Maybe you know where that was invented, too. Tell me when I get home.

Buster

an "The Brain" Powers
2 Oak Street
Elwood City

"I play the accordion a little,"
said Buster. "But your accordion has
a lot more buttons than mine."

"And every button can make
two sounds," said Robert.
"One sound is made when you push
the instrument in, and another is made
when you pull it out.
You have to practice a lot."

"That's what I keep telling myself,"
said Buster. "But I don't always listen."

"When I practice," Buster added,
"I get nervous if anyone is listening.
Do you get nervous performing in front
of big crowds?"

"Sometimes," said Robert.
"But when I get nervous,
I pretend people aren't there.
I'm just at my house, you know,
practicing by myself."

TUCKER

Dear Mom,

I met Robert at a music festival called the Conjunto Heritage Taller. He has six accordions and a big collection of hats. Don't worry, I won't buy any extra accordions. One is more than enough for me.

Buster

P.S. But maybe I'll buy a hat.

Mom Baxter
5 Willow Way
Elwood City

Buster met Robert's sister, Cristina.
She played the accordion, too.

"My accordion is named Beatrice," said Buster. "What's yours called?"

"Nobody names their accordion," said Cristina.

"Oh," said Buster.

HI! I'M
EATRICE

HI, I'M
MATT

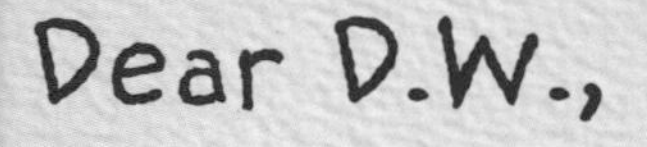

Dear D.W.,

Robert and Cristina
have a dog that's
91 years old
(in dog years). Just
think how many
accordions he's
heard in all that
time! I wonder
if he's ever howled
along with them.

Buster

Robert showed Buster
all the different hats he wore
when he played.

It was important to pick the right hat
for the right mood.

Dear Binky,

Robert has some accordions that are older than our parents. They are in really good shape (the accordions, I mean).

Buster

Later, Robert and Rudy took Buster to a restaurant.
He got a special look in the kitchen.

The cook was making tacos.
First, he rolled the dough into flat circles.
Then he fried them on both sides.

"It smells really good in here,"
Buster said hungrily.

"My favorite taco is country and egg,"
said Rudy.

"Mine is potato and egg,"
said Robert. "I add salt and pepper
to spice it up a bit."

Buster was counting on the menu.
"They make twenty-two different kinds
of tacos here," he said.
"I wonder if they would make up
a special one."

TACOS
HOUSE SPECIAL
PIZZA TACO
HOT
AND BEAN
COUNTRY AND EGG
POTATO AND EGG
CHICKEN
MEAT AND EGG
GUACAMOLE
ELIZA'S
BEAN AND
BEEF ONION
CARNITAS

Dear Francine,

I had a guacamole-and-bean taco today. I may order a pizza taco tomorrow.

I might be the first person ever to eat a pizza taco.

If I get famous, I will let you know.

Buster

blue

SAN ANTONIO
PM
FEB 4
TX
Francine
Maple Drive Apt.
Elwood City

That night Buster practiced
for a long time on his accordion.

He even called Arthur to play for him
over the phone.

"So, how was I?" Buster asked.

"Well," said Arthur, "you're not ready
to play for a thousand people who
love accordion music, that's for sure."

Later, after Buster fell asleep,
he dreamed about playing
the accordion in the festival.
But the accordion turned into
a monster with eight arms.

When Buster woke up,
he put the accordion
in the closet
and shut the door tight.

The next day Buster took his mind off the accordion for a while.

He and his father strolled along the Riverwalk, looking at all the restaurants and shops.

"So much food," said Buster, "and so little time."

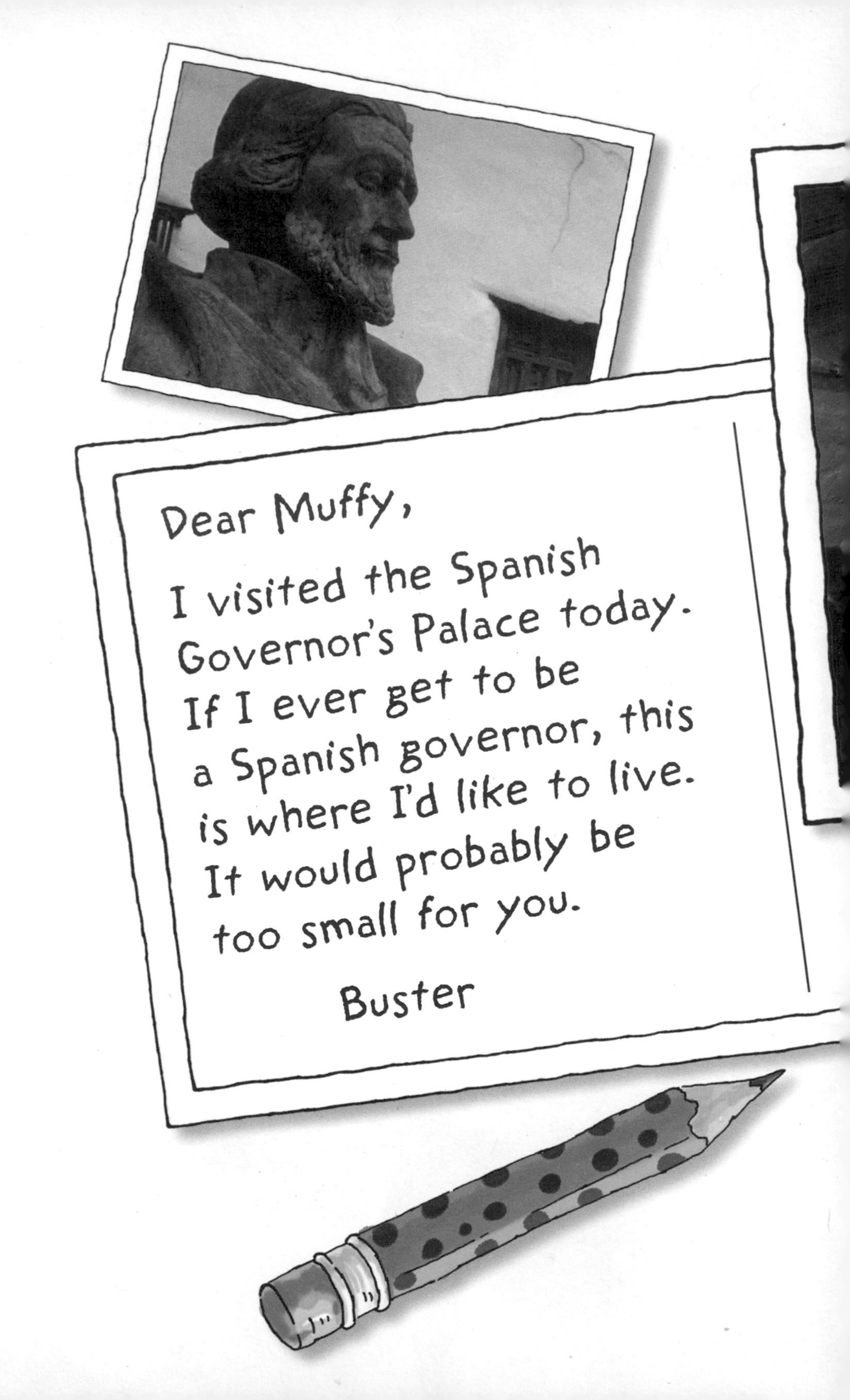

Dear Muffy,

I visited the Spanish Governor's Palace today. If I ever get to be a Spanish governor, this is where I'd like to live. It would probably be too small for you.

Buster

At the Accordion Festival,
Buster and his father
mixed with the crowd.

"There are lots of people here,"
said Mr. Baxter.

"And there are lots of accordions, too,"
said Buster. "Just think, Dad,
we'll see the best players from
around the world.
Maybe I can pick up some pointers."

Dear Arthur,

I loved listening to everyone play at the festival. Maybe when I get good enough, I can play here, too. This will take a while.

Buster

When Robert took the stage,
Buster clapped with everyone else.
He started to count how many people
were in the audience.

"One . . . two . . . three . . ."

But once Robert started playing,
Buster got lost in the music.

Dear Arthur,

Robert was a big hit at the festival. Afterward, he signed autographs and lots of fans took his picture.

Nobody asked for my autograph or took my picture. Who knows what they would have done if I had played for them?

Buster

On the plane home,
Buster took out his accordion.

"I promised Robert
I'd keep practicing," he said.
"Maybe I should start right now."

"How much practice do you think
you'll need?" asked his father.

"Hours and hours," said Buster,
"but we've got plenty of time."

"Oh," said his father,
and put on his headphones
before starting the engines.

Arthur Read
00 Main Street
Elwood City

Dear Robert,

I've been playing
my accordion
a lot lately.

My friends all say
I used to sound much worse.

Maybe some day you can
hear me play without worrying
about hurting your ears!

Buster